Grumpy Bear

Best Friend Bear

Secret Bear

This book belongs to:

Marty Butler

Wish Bear

Love-a-lot Bear

Published by Scholastic Inc.
90 Old Sherman Turnpike, Danbury, CT 06816.

SCHOLASTIC and associated logos are trademarks and/or registered trademarks of Scholastic Inc.

ISBN 0-439-79990-2

Printed in the U.S.A.

First Scholastic Printing, November 2005

The Day Nobody Shared

by Nancy Parent
& Quinlan B. Lee

Illustrated by
Jay Johnson &
Rivoli Design Group

SCHOLASTIC INC.

New York   Toronto   London   Auckland   Sydney
Mexico City   New Delhi   Hong Kong   Buenos Aires

One day, Good Luck Bear got a box of rainbow bars in the mail.

He decided to hide
the treats so he could
have them all to himself.

"I'm hiding my rainbow bars so I don't have to share them," Good Luck Bear whispered.

"But it feels so good to share," said Share Bear.

"It does?"

asked Good Luck Bear.

10

"Come for a ride on the swings," said Share Bear. "I'll tell you a story called *The Day Nobody Shared...*"

. . . Once upon a time, Cheer Bear made a giant
ice-cream sundae with rainbow sprinkles that she
wouldn't share with any of her friends.

Cheer Bear ended up with an awful tummy ache
from eating the ice cream all by herself.

Then Bedtime Bear refused to share his special spot to watch the Care-a-lot parade.

But without Grumpy Bear to keep Bedtime Bear awake, he fell asleep and missed the whole thing!

Hooray for Care Bears

That afternoon, Tenderheart Bear wouldn't share his toys, so nobody wanted to play with him.

Tenderheart Bear quickly got bored.
"Toys don't laugh and talk like friends,"
he said unhappily.

Later, Love-a-lot Bear wouldn't share her kite with Funshine Bear, so he played with Wish Bear instead.

Even *Secret Bear's* picnic was ruined. It started
to rain, and *Secret Bear* wouldn't share her umbrella
with the others.

All of the treats got gooey, and no one
was able to eat them. . . .
Share Bear's voice trailed off.

Good Luck Bear said,
"What bad luck that no one
wanted to share,"

"That's right,"
said Share Bear.

"If I share my rainbow bars," Good Luck Bear asked, "will that make everyone happy?"

"Yes," said Share Bear.

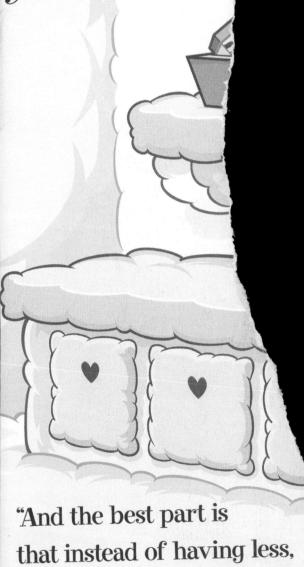

Sharing takes ha

"And the best part is
that instead of having less,
you end up with more."

bars with
ck Bear.
and added,

"We can throw a sharing party in the park!"

27

Share Bear and
Good Luck Bear ran
to share the good news.

They invited all of
their friends to the
sharing party.

Everyone brought something fun to share.

"I can't wait to share in the fun!" said Funshine Bear, laughing.

When they passed
Share Bear's house, Share
Bear ran inside and came
out with a bunch
of balloons.

"I'm going to share these!" said Share Bear.

"It feels really great to share," said Good Luck Bear.

34

"And it tastes yummy, too!"
added Bedtime Bear.

"Of course," said Share Bear.

"Everything is sweeter when it's shared
with a friend."

How Can You Share Like Share Bear?

In the beginning, Good Luck Bear didn't want to share his rainbow bars.

💜 What things are hard for you to share?

💜 Why?

The day nobody shared wasn't a fun day at all.

💜 Why not?

💜 How do you feel when someone won't share with you?

Think of a time when you shared something.

- ❤ How did you feel?
- ❤ Were you glad you shared?
- ❤ How do you think it made the other person feel?

Bashful Heart Bear

Cheer Bear

Share Bear

Bedtime Bear

Funshine Bear